Vampire Baby

There are more books about the Bailey City Monsters!

#1 The Monsters Next Door

#2 Howling at the Hauntlys'

#3 Vampire Trouble

#4 Kilmer's Pet Monster

#5 Double Trouble Monsters

#6 Spooky Spells

#7 Vampire Baby

Super Special #1: The Hauntlys' Hairy Surprise

Coming soon

#8 Snow Monster Mystery

Vampire Baby

by Marcia Thornton Jones
and
Debbie Dadey

illustrated by John Steven Gurney

A
LITTLE APPLE
PAPERBACK

SCHOLASTIC INC.
New York   Toronto   London   Auckland   Sydney
Mexico City   New Delhi   Hong Kong

ISBN 0-439-05872-4

Text copyright © 1999 by Marcia Thornton Jones and Debra S. Dadey.
Illustrations copyright © 1999 by Scholastic Inc.
All rights reserved. Published by Scholastic Inc.
SCHOLASTIC, APPLE PAPERBACKS, and associated logos
are trademarks of Scholastic Inc.
THE BAILEY CITY MONSTERS in design is a registered
trademark of Scholastic Inc.

12 11 10 9 8 7 6 5 4 3 2 1   9/9 0 1 2 3 4/0

Printed in the U.S.A.   40

First Scholastic printing, August 1999

Contents

1. Bathilda   1
2. Dracula's Daughter   8
3. Midnight   15
4. Bat Wrestling   22
5. Vampire Bites   27
6. Chewy   33
7. Vampire Trap   40
8. Monster's Midnight Snack   47
9. A Plan   52
10. Chasing Bathilda   56
11. The Real Vampire   61
12. Dracula   66

1
Bathilda

"What happened to you?" Ben asked as soon as Jane plopped on the floor of their tree house. "You look terrible."

Jane yawned. She looked like she hadn't slept in days. Deep circles underlined her eyes and her black hair was so tangled it stuck up in crazy angles. She wore an orange sweater, but all the buttons were fastened wrong.

Ben's sister, Annie, patted Jane on the shoulder. "Maybe you're coming down with a cold."

"I was shaking all night," Jane said, "but it wasn't from a cold. Didn't you hear those horrible noises?"

"I didn't hear a thing," Annie said.

"All I heard was Annie snoring," Ben

said. "That's probably what you heard, too."

Annie punched Ben on the arm. "It was not. I don't even snore."

"Whatever it was, I thought it would never stop," Jane said. "I didn't sleep a wink."

"What did it sound like?" Annie asked.

"It sounded like a cross between a baby crying and a monster shrieking. And," Jane said, leaning close, "I think it came from Hauntly Manor Inn."

The kids looked at the house at 13 Dedman Street and shuddered. They could remember when the house next door to them was brand-new, but then the Hauntlys moved in and hung a sign in the yard that said HAUNTLY MANOR INN. Now the shutters were at odd angles, the paint was peeling, and the sidewalk was lined with jagged cracks. The inn looked exactly like a haunted house. Even the grass and trees had withered and died.

Just then, the door to Hauntly Manor Inn

creaked open and Kilmer Hauntly pushed something big and black down the warped steps of the porch. Kilmer was in the same fourth-grade class as Ben and Jane, but he didn't look like a normal fourth-grader. He was a head taller than all the other kids and his clothes were at least two sizes too small. His hair was cut straight across the top of his head. Some kids thought he looked just like Frankenstein's monster.

Ben, Annie, and Jane scrambled down from the tree house and hurried to meet their friend. "What is that black thing?" Ben asked as he jogged up the sidewalk to Hauntly Manor Inn.

"It looks like an old-fashioned baby buggy," Annie said.

Kilmer nodded as his friends gathered in front of him. "You are right," he told Annie. "This carriage has been in my family for ages."

Everything about the carriage was black. Even the handles and wheels were black. It looked exactly like a tiny hearse. A

shiny piece of black fabric was even draped over the bed.

"Why are you pushing an ancient baby buggy around?" Ben asked.

"Because," Kilmer said with a grin, "we have a new visitor at our inn." Kilmer reached over the buggy's hood to draw back the long black fabric. "I would like to introduce you to my cousin Bathilda!"

Ben, Jane, and Annie looked inside the buggy. Bathilda was snuggled inside a black

5

blanket, but she smiled when she saw the three faces peering in at her.

Bathilda wasn't very old, but Annie noticed the baby already had two new eye-teeth. Bathilda's black hair grew down in a point on her pasty white forehead. "Isn't she cute?" Annie said and stuck her finger inside the carriage to tickle Bathilda's pale cheek.

"Ouch!" Annie jerked her hand away when Bathilda tried to bite it.

"Babies put everything in their mouths," Kilmer told Annie as he carefully spread the black fabric over the buggy again.

"Why do you keep her covered up like that?" Ben asked. "It's not even cold out here."

Kilmer glanced at the cloudless sky. "The sun is too bright," Kilmer said. "It must not touch her delicate skin," he told them as he started pushing the buggy down the sidewalk. "The trip has been up-setting to Bathilda, so Mother suggested I take the buggy for a ride down Dedman Street."

Ben, Annie, and Jane followed their friend and his buggy. "When did Bathilda get here?" Jane asked. "I don't remember seeing anybody arrive."

Kilmer nodded. "My uncle flew in last night and dropped off Bathilda. He won't be back for a while so you'll be seeing lots of Bathilda!"

"I hope baby-sitting doesn't get in the way of playing soccer," Ben griped.

Annie pulled on Jane's arm to make her slow down. When Annie was sure Ben and Kilmer were far enough ahead so they couldn't hear, she leaned close to Jane and whispered, "Normal babies don't appear overnight."

"They do at the Hauntlys'," Jane told her, "but I have a feeling that Bathilda is no ordinary baby!"

2

Dracula's Daughter

"This is a dumb thing to do," Ben complained the next day as he followed Jane and Annie up the sidewalk to Hauntly Manor Inn.

Jane shook her head. "My mother said it was polite to bring a toy for a new baby."

"A toy is one thing," Ben said, "but a doll is something else. Why didn't you get a soccer ball?"

"Because Bathilda is a baby," Annie said as the three friends climbed the steps to the porch. "She can't play soccer."

Ben, Annie, and Jane had to wipe away cobwebs dangling from the porch roof. Then they stepped around the black baby buggy sitting in the middle of the porch.

"The Hauntlys shouldn't leave that

buggy out all night," Annie said. "Something could happen to it."

"It looks like something already did," Jane said. She was right. The carriage was definitely lopsided. Jane bent down and pointed to one of the tires. "Here's the problem. This tire is flat."

"You should've bought Bathilda a new set of wheels instead of a silly doll," Ben said as he lifted the tarnished door knocker and let it fall with a loud thud.

Heavy footsteps thumped down the hall inside Hauntly Manor Inn and the door slowly creaked open. Kilmer's dad, Boris Hauntly, peered down at the three visitors and grinned.

The kids knew Boris Hauntly was friendly, but every time they saw his gleaming white eyeteeth, goose bumps appeared across their arms. Boris always wore a long black cape that fastened at his throat with a huge bloodred button. If it wasn't for his red hair, Boris Hauntly could have been Dracula's twin brother.

"We came to visit Bathilda," Annie said.

"Welcome," Boris said in his thick Transylvanian accent. "Do come in." Boris held the door open and the kids silently walked inside Hauntly Manor Inn.

Thick bloodred drapes covered all the windows so little sunlight ever reached inside Hauntly Manor Inn. Cobwebs clung to every corner, and a thick layer of dust blanketed every piece of furniture.

Kilmer's mother, Hilda Hauntly, appeared at the top of the curving staircase and smiled down at the kids. "How nice of you to come," she said. "Kilmer is in Bathilda's room."

Kilmer's mother was a scientist and she always wore a white lab coat covered with strange stains. The kids on Dedman Street were sure she was a mad scientist who stirred up unusual concoctions in her secret laboratory.

"It is right this way," Boris said. His cape fluttered from his shoulders like giant bat wings as he led the way up the steps and

11

down the darkened hallway. "My niece is so perfect," Boris said as he walked ahead of them. "She looks exactly like my brother. She's a chip off the old block!"

"Boris looks just like Dracula," Jane whispered to Annie. "Do you know what that means?"

Annie shook her head.

"It means Bathilda could be Dracula's very own daughter!" Jane hissed.

Annie couldn't answer because just then Boris opened a heavy wooden door. Ben, Jane, and Annie stopped in the doorway of Bathilda's room to let their eyes adjust to the deep shadows. Black curtains covering the windows blended with the black paint on the walls. Bathilda's room was so dark it looked like a deep cave. The only thing that wasn't black was her crib bedding. It was the color of blood. A mobile with bats dangled over her crib.

Annie jumped back when she saw a giant spider hanging on its silvery web over Bathilda. Annie knew all about Kilmer's pet

spiders, but she still didn't like the looks of the hairy creatures. Bathilda didn't seem to mind. As soon as she saw the spider she pointed and giggled so that Annie could see her baby eyeteeth.

Kilmer sat in a rocking chair. He was in the middle of reading a story about witches to Bathilda, but he stopped when he saw his friends. "I am so glad you came," Kilmer told them.

"We brought Bathilda a present," Annie said and gently placed the doll in the crib.

Bathilda laughed, showing her pointy eyeteeth. She grabbed it and, before anybody could stop her, Bathilda bit the doll right on its neck.

3
Midnight

Ben crouched low, making sure Annie and Jane couldn't see him sneaking up behind the couch. It was almost midnight, and Jane was having a sleepover with Annie.

Annie and Jane were busy watching scary movies. Eerie scenes of haunted houses, vampires, and monsters flashed on the television screen. They didn't notice Ben as he slithered across the den floor. Slowly, he reached up, his hands like claws. Just as a witch flew across the television screen, Ben made his move.

"Boo!" he said and grabbed Annie's and Jane's necks. Jane gasped, but Annie let out a bloodcurdling scream.

"Shhh!" Ben warned as he clamped his

hand over Annie's mouth. "Do you want to get us in trouble?"

Annie flung Ben's hand away and nodded. "You deserve to be grounded until you're sixty-two," she snapped. "You scared us to death!"

Ben grinned. "I was just having a little fun," he told her. "Besides, I bet Mom doesn't know you're watching this movie."

"She also doesn't know you're bothering us," Annie told her brother. "But I'm going to tell unless you leave us alone!"

Ben turned to go, but when he did, something caught his eye. "That's odd," he said, walking to the window. "All the lights are on at Hauntly Manor Inn." Jane and Annie hurried over to Ben as he unlatched the window and slid it open. "Listen," he said.

Cold chills exploded on their arms and necks when a screech echoed across the yard. It sounded like it came straight from Hauntly Manor Inn.

"What could that be?" Annie asked with a shiver.

"There's only one way to find out," Ben told her, sliding the window shut.

"We're not going out there," Annie told Ben.

"We have to," Ben said. "Something may be wrong at the Hauntlys'. It's up to us to help them."

Jane looked at Annie as another scream from Hauntly Manor Inn cut through the night. "Ben's right," Jane said. "Meet me at the back door in ten minutes!"

The three kids slipped into jeans and sweatshirts. Ben found his binoculars and they all grabbed flashlights. Just as the hallway clock struck midnight, they slipped out the back door into a night as black as the walls in Bathilda's room.

A cold wind shook the red leaves on the maple tree, and somewhere a dog howled. Annie pulled her sweatshirt tight and shivered. "Are you sure this is a good idea?"

she asked. "Whatever is screaming might not want us to find it."

"We'll stay in the shadows," Ben told her. "It won't even see us."

"I hope you're right," Jane whispered as the three kids pushed their way through an opening in the bushes that separated Ben and Annie's yard from Hauntly Manor Inn. The wind seemed colder as it rattled the dead branches of the trees. Deep shadows covered the entire yard. Jane led her friends around the side of the inn. They looked in every window they passed.

"I can't see a thing," Annie whispered. "Maybe we were just imagining it."

Just then another blood-chilling scream erupted from somewhere inside Hauntly Manor. The kids couldn't tell where it came from.

"Follow me," Jane told her friends. She led them to the maple tree and they all scrambled up to the tree house.

"There," Annie said, pointing to an up-

stairs window. "It looks like it's a Hauntly reunion!"

Ben used his binoculars to get a close-up view. "It's just Boris and Hilda, but they're covered with white stuff," he told Annie and Jane. "I bet it's vampire blood."

"Why would vampires have white blood?" Annie asked.

Ben shrugged. "How would I know? I've never actually asked a vampire for a blood sample. It could be buzzard brains or rattlesnake intestines from one of Hilda's creations."

"Who's screaming?" Jane asked.

Ben shook his head. "I don't know, but the Hauntlys look really upset."

All of a sudden, Ben gasped. "Quick, hide!" Ben told them. "They're coming outside and they're heading straight for us."

4
Bat Wrestling

"I thought we were goners," Jane admitted the next morning. She threw a baseball to Annie. "I'm just glad Boris and Hilda didn't see us last night."

Annie caught the ball and looked across her backyard to Hauntly Manor Inn. "Don't you think it's strange that the Hauntlys carried Bathilda up and down the sidewalk at exactly midnight?"

Ben shrugged. "People do weird things to make babies sleep. Aunt Thelma drove Buster around in the car until he fell asleep."

Annie threw the ball to Ben and nodded. "I guess you're right, but what about that white stuff the Hauntlys had all over them?"

"I can answer that," Jane said. "I bet that

was baby cereal. It's white and sticky and pretty disgusting."

"How would you know?" Ben asked.

Jane caught the ball that Ben threw and passed it on to Annie. "You're not the only one that has cousins, you know."

"Do vampires eat cereal?" Annie asked, missing the ball. "It might clog up their bloodsucking fangs."

Ben grabbed the ball and threw it, but he didn't aim very well. The ball sailed into the Hauntlys' front yard. Jane raced after it and found the ball underneath a dead tree.

Suddenly Annie and Ben heard Jane's screams. They looked at each other and ran over to find out what was wrong. Jane was busy swatting a huge black bat. It was so large it covered Jane's head. "Get it off me!" Jane yelled.

Ben and Annie wrestled with the large bat until they finally pulled it away from Jane. Jane fell on the ground, gasping for air. "Are you okay?" Annie said, dropping beside her friend.

Ben laughed out loud and squeezed the huge bat.

"I'm glad you think my almost dying was funny," Jane said, giving Ben a dirty look.

"Why are you still holding that disgusting thing?" Annie asked.

Ben laughed again. "Kilmer might get mad at me for ruining Bathilda's swing." Ben held up the bat. For the first time the girls noticed the rope attached to the bat. It was a very strange bat swing, just the right size for a baby.

Jane shuddered. "I'm getting out of

here." She jumped up and raced over to the tree house. Annie followed her friend. Ben came, too, laughing all the way.

"I have a very strange feeling about Bathilda," Jane said. "She is not a normal baby."

"What do you expect?" Ben asked. "She's a Hauntly. Nothing is normal about the Hauntlys."

Annie didn't say anything. She frowned, thinking about Bathilda's pointy eyeteeth, the cavelike bedroom, and the way Bathilda bit the doll's neck. Finally Annie blurted, "I don't think Bathilda is a normal baby, either. In fact, I think she's a vampire baby!"

Jane and Ben laughed, but they didn't get a chance to answer because suddenly the entire tree started shaking.

"Hang on for your lives!" Ben yelled.

5

Vampire Bites

The tree shook. Branches swayed. Leaves rained down on Ben, Jane, and Annie. Suddenly Kilmer popped his head into the tree house. "Who wants to go to Burger Doodle?" he asked.

"I do!" Ben shouted, quickly climbing down the tree after Kilmer. Jane and Annie followed.

"Let's take our bikes," Jane suggested. "It'll be faster."

Ben and Annie went into the garage to get their bikes. Annie hopped on her bike, but Ben pushed his bike out. "You aren't going to push your bike the whole way, are you?" Jane teased Ben.

Ben frowned. "I can't take my bike. My tires are flat. I guess I ran over tacks."

Jane bent down to look at Ben's tires.

27

She put her finger over two tiny puncture marks. "I don't think tacks did that," Jane whispered to Annie. "I think Bathilda is to blame. These look just like a vampire's bite. Maybe you were right about her."

Kilmer didn't notice Annie and Jane whispering. "That's okay," he told Ben. "We'll all walk to Burger Doodle. Wait a minute and I'll be right back." Kilmer disappeared inside Hauntly Manor Inn. In just a few minutes he reappeared with a little bundle, which he put inside the black baby carriage.

Kilmer pushed the baby carriage over to the kids. "I might as well take Bathilda for a walk."

"That's very nice of you," Jane said, peeking inside the carriage. Bathilda was busy shaking a rattle. It wasn't an ordinary baby rattle, though. This rattle looked like a big, hairy spider.

Kilmer pushed the carriage along as the kids walked down Dedman Street toward

Forest Lane. "I thought the buggy's wheels were flat," Ben said. "Did you fix them?"

Kilmer nodded. "I'm an expert at patching tires. I've had lots of practice. I could help you fix your bike tires, too."

"Thanks," Ben said.

As the kids turned the corner and headed toward Burger Doodle, Ben saw a huge dog. "Look at the size of that dog!" he said.

Annie gulped when she saw the Great Dane sitting in front of Burger Doodle. It was nearly as tall as she was and its gaping mouth looked like it could swallow her head with one giant gulp. "Do you think he's friendly?" Annie asked. The dog must have understood because he put his nose on the sidewalk, whined, and covered his head with his paws.

"He looks okay to me," Ben said, walking past the dog and going inside Burger Doodle. "I'd like to know who that dog belongs to. Maybe they'd let me play with him."

"I don't want to play with him," Annie

30

admitted. "He's so big, I'd be afraid he might bite my arm off."

"Just because he's big doesn't mean he's mean," Ben said. "I wish Mom would let us have a dog."

"All I want is a Doodlegum milk shake," Jane said. The kids went up to the counter and ordered tall shakes while Kilmer gave Bathilda a tiny red bottle. Bathilda sucked on the bottle so loudly everyone in the restaurant turned around and smiled.

A third-grade girl named Carey skipped over to see Bathilda. "I just love babies," Carey squealed, peeking inside the baby buggy. Bathilda giggled and tossed her spider rattle right at Carey's head. Then Bathilda smiled so broadly that Carey saw the baby's new eyeteeth.

Carey backed away and shrieked, "Oh, my gosh! What's wrong with that baby?"

The kids jumped out of her way as Carey raced out of Burger Doodle, grabbed the collar of the Great Dane, and hurried out of sight.

6

Chewy

"Carey looked like she had just seen a two-headed monster," Ben said with a laugh. He sat on the floor of the tree house talking to Jane and Annie.

Jane giggled. "I'll never forget the funny look she had on her face."

"I hope Carey forgets about Bathilda," Annie said softly. "Carey could cause a lot of trouble for the Hauntlys."

"Carey IS a lot of trouble," Ben agreed. Carey's father was the president of Bailey City Bank and Carey was used to getting everything she wanted.

Jane looked out of the tree house and pointed. "Here comes trouble now."

Carey rode down the sidewalk on her brand-new, super-duper purple bike. The huge Great Dane they had seen at Burger Doodle ran alongside her.

"That's not fair," Ben snapped. "Carey already has a cat. I don't even have one pet."

Carey parked her bicycle beside Ben's house and marched under the tree house. "Hel-looo!" Carey yelled.

Ben put his finger to his lips and the kids sat perfectly still. "You can't fool me," Carey yelled. "I know you're up there!"

Annie shrugged and peeked over the tree house rail. "Hi, Carey," she said.

Carey waved up at Annie. "I just came to see what's happening with that weird baby."

Ben popped his head over the rail and changed the subject. "Where'd you get the dog?"

Carey petted the big dog's head. "This is Chewy," she bragged. "He's the best-behaved dog in the whole world."

"Why'd you name him Chewy?" Jane asked, looking over the rail. "That seems like a funny name for a dog."

Carey's face turned red. "He liked to chew when he was little, but he doesn't do that anymore." Carey petted the big dog again, and he perked up his ears.

"Woof!" the dog barked and bounded toward the Hauntlys' house.

"Come back here!" Carey yelled to Chewy, but he didn't pay any attention.

"He doesn't look very well behaved to me," Ben teased.

"Oh, my gosh!" Annie screamed. "Chewy is heading straight for Bathilda and Kilmer!"

The four kids rushed over to the Hauntlys' porch. When they got there, Kilmer was petting Chewy's head and Bathilda was trying to chew on Chewy's tail.

"Are you okay?" Jane asked Kilmer. "We were afraid Chewy was going to eat you guys alive."

Carey sniffed. "I told you Chewy was very well behaved. He wouldn't hurt a flea. Now let me see that baby again." Carey

pushed Chewy out of the way and peeked inside the buggy.

Bathilda was snuggling a stuffed rat, but as soon as Carey leaned over, Bathilda pushed away the rat and grabbed Carey's curly hair. Bathilda pulled Carey closer and closer until she was close enough to try and bite Carey's nose.

"Help!" Carey screamed. She jerked away, but Bathilda hung onto Carey's curls. A clump of blond hair stayed in Bathilda's hand when Carey finally pulled free. "Save me from that little monster!" Carey screamed and ran away from the porch, with Chewy racing beside her.

"I'm glad she's gone," Ben said.

"Me too," Kilmer agreed. "She's always screaming about something."

Just then, Carey screamed again. Ben nodded. "I know what you mean."

"Come on," Annie said. "We'd better go see what's wrong."

Ben rolled his eyes. "She probably just broke a fingernail." Ben, Annie, and Jane walked over to the tree to see what was wrong with Carey. Kilmer stayed on the porch with Bathilda.

"Look at my tires!" Carey screeched. "They're ruined!" Sure enough, both of Carey's tires were flat. Jane looked closely. They had two puncture marks in each tire, just like Ben's.

"That's too bad," Annie said.

Carey shook her finger at the kids. "I'm going to find out who's responsible! I wouldn't be surprised if that baby had something to do with this." Carey pushed her bike away, with Chewy trotting along behind her.

"There could be big trouble if Carey tells her father there's something batty about Bathilda," Annie admitted.

"We have no proof that Bathilda is anything more than a sweet baby," Jane said. "After all, Bathilda can't even walk yet."

"Vampires don't have to walk," Annie pointed out. "They fly. Vampire babies could be just like bats. Maybe they're born able to fly and bite. And if a vampire baby is anything like a real baby, we could be in serious trouble."

"Why?" Jane asked.

"Because babies eat all day long. Bathilda may be on the prowl for fresh blood!" Annie said.

Ben looked up at the darkening sky. "Nighttime is the perfect time for a vampire baby to stalk Dedman Street."

Annie didn't say any more. Instead, she pulled her collar around her neck and shivered.

7
Vampire Trap

"This has gone too far," Ben sputtered the next afternoon in his backyard. He held up his soccer ball so Annie could see. It was as flat as a pancake.

"Let me see that," Annie said, grabbing it from Ben. She slowly turned it over. "Just as I thought," Annie said. "It has two holes in it."

"Whoever used my soccer ball as a pincushion better watch out," Ben yelled.

Jane jogged up to the yard just as Ben yelled. She saw the ball in Annie's hand. "Yours isn't the only one," Jane told Ben and held out her own soccer ball. It was as flat as Ben's.

"It looks like soccer is a game Bathilda can really sink her teeth into," Annie said seriously.

"Something has to be done," Jane said. "We can't let a batty baby suck the air out of Dedman Street."

"We don't know for sure that Bathilda is responsible," Ben told her. "Maybe there's a wild rattlesnake slithering around Dedman Street. Or it could be a crazy grandma with knitting needles on the loose," he joked.

"There are no rattlesnakes in Bailey City," Annie said. "Besides, nothing went flat before Bathilda came to visit."

"You have to admit," Jane said, "a baby with fangs is pretty suspicious. Remember how she tried to suck the blood out of that doll we gave her?"

"That explains why your head is empty," Ben said with a laugh. "Bathilda must have sucked your brains dry!"

Jane pointed a finger at Ben's chest. "My brain is perfectly fine," she said. "In fact, I have an idea."

Ben rolled his eyes. "Look out, world,"

he teased. "Run for your lives! Jane has an idea!"

Jane curled her fingers into a fist and held them in front of Ben's nose. "I'll make you a deal," she told Ben. "If you go along with me, I won't make your nose as flat as your soccer ball!"

Annie reached out and grabbed Jane's fist. "Go where?" she asked.

"On a little spying mission. I'm going to catch Bathilda in the act."

"Vampires come out at night," Ben said. "Are you sure you want to go on a vampire hunt in the dead of night?"

"We have to do something," Jane said, "before Carey beats us to it. Unless you're too chicken."

"I'm not scared," Ben said. "I'll do it if you will."

Jane nodded. "We'll meet under the tree house at midnight," she told her friends. "Be sure to fix your soccer ball and bring it with you."

"Why?" Ben asked. "Are you planning a midnight game?"

Jane shook her head. "Just do it," she said.

That night, Ben and Annie sneaked outside. A full moon hung low in the sky and the branches of the maple tree cast eerie shadows across the yard.

Jane was already waiting for them. "Follow me," she whispered.

The three kids stayed in the shadows as they sneaked into the Hauntlys' yard. Jane quietly left her soccer ball at the back door of Hauntly Manor Inn. Then she grabbed Ben's soccer ball. She placed it halfway between the door and their tree house.

"What are you doing?" Annie hissed.

"If we plan to catch Bathilda in the act," Jane said, "we have to set a trap. These balls will lead her straight to us."

"What will we do with her if we catch her?" Annie whimpered to her friends after they settled on the floor of the tree house.

Jane shrugged. "We won't do anything. We just need to find out for sure that it's Bathilda."

"If she's really a vampire baby, wouldn't she bite people's necks and not soccer balls?" Ben asked.

"Babies will chew on anything," Jane said. "Especially vampire babies!"

A chill wind whipped through the tree's branches and leaves drifted down to settle on the floor as the kids waited. A dog

45

howled in the distance and a screech owl hooted from the Hauntlys' backyard.

"Maybe this isn't such a good idea," Annie finally said as she covered her throat with her collar. "If Bathilda really is a baby vampire, she could swoop up here and suck our blood."

"Don't tell me you're scared of an itsy-bitsy baby," Ben said with a snicker.

"Black widow spiders are itsy-bitsy," Annie pointed out, "but their bite can be deadly."

Jane felt something crawl up her pant leg. She swatted at it. "Annie's right," Jane said. "This wasn't a good idea. Let's go home before we're eaten alive!"

Just as they got ready to scramble out of the tree house, Ben, Annie, and Jane heard something that made them freeze.

8

Monster's Midnight Snack

Annie whimpered. Jane shivered. Ben gulped. Something panted in huge raspy breaths at the base of the tree.

"Is it a vampire?" Jane cried softly.

"It sounds more like a monster to me," Ben moaned.

"Either way," Annie said, "you're about to be a midnight snack."

"Not if it eats you first," Ben said, dodging behind his sister.

Jane tried to hide behind Ben. Annie scrambled to get behind them both. They all froze when they heard claws scraping on the bark of the tree.

"It's coming to get us!" Annie shrieked as the three kids huddled in a corner.

Just then, a light flooded the tree house.

Ben, Annie, and Jane shielded their eyes against the bright beam of a flashlight.

"Just as I thought," a familiar voice snapped. "I knew you three were hiding up here."

"It's not a monster," Jane said with a big whoosh of air. "It's only Carey."

"She's even worse," Ben muttered.

"What are you doing here?" Annie asked Carey.

"There's something strange going on at that monster motel next door," Carey told them, "and I came to find out what it was. I should have known that you three would be in the middle of it all!"

"But we weren't doing anything," Annie argued.

"We'll see about that," Carey told her. Then she disappeared down the ladder.

"We have to catch her before she does something stupid," Jane gasped.

"Too late," Ben told her. "Everything Carey does is stupid." But Ben followed Annie and Jane down the ladder. A dark

48

shadow swooped between the branches of the tree, but the kids were too worried about Carey to notice.

Carey stood at the bottom of the tree house. Chewy bounded around her, trying to grab the flat soccer balls she held in each hand. "You're the ones who ruined my bicycle tires," Carey sputtered when Ben, Jane, and Annie climbed out of the tree. "These balls prove it! I'm going to tell my dad on you! When he finds out you ruined my bicycle's tires, you'll be sorry."

"You've got it all wrong!" Annie blurted. "We didn't touch your tires."

"Those flat soccer balls don't prove a thing," Jane added. "After all, we wouldn't punch holes in our own balls."

Carey threw the ruined balls onto the ground and Chewy grabbed one. He ran circles around Carey, but she didn't pay attention to her dog. She put her hands on her hips and glared at Ben, Annie, and Jane. "I don't believe a word you say!"

"But we didn't do it!" Annie said. "Bathilda did!"

Jane and Ben both pounced on Annie and tried to cover her mouth. But it was too late. The words were already out.

"I knew there was something strange about that baby. Now I know what it is. Bathilda is a vampire baby. That Hauntly family is history in Bailey City!" Carey said with an evil laugh. "My dad will see to that!" Carey grabbed Chewy's collar and pulled him down Dedman Street toward her mansion.

"I feel terrible," Annie moaned. "The Hauntlys are about to be run out of town and it's all my fault!"

9
A Plan

The kids sat in the tree house the next morning playing with action figures. Ben threw one out of the tree house to see where it landed. "I feel terrible," Annie said.

"You look rotten, too," Ben teased, throwing another figure to the ground. "Kaboom!"

Annie ignored Ben and turned to Jane. "What are we going to do about Bathilda?" she asked.

"Do?" Ben said. "Why do we have to do anything? Except for a few flat balls and tires everything is okay. Why can't we just go on with our lives like everything is hunky-dory?"

"Because it isn't," Jane said. "We have to think of a plan to help Bathilda before Carey does something drastic."

Ben torpedoed another action figure over the rail. "Look out below!" he yelled.

"Ouch!" came a shout from the ground.

An evil grin came over Ben's face. "Ooops," he said. "Maybe if I'm lucky I hit Carey."

Annie peeked over the side. "No, you just hit Kilmer on the head."

Ben shrugged. "That's okay. Kilmer has the hardest head of anybody I know."

Kilmer climbed into the tree house and Ben apologized. "Sorry," Ben said. "I didn't know you were down there."

Kilmer shrugged. "That's okay, it didn't hurt much. What are you doing up here?"

Annie sighed. "We're trying to think of a way to help Bathilda."

Kilmer had a puzzled look on his face. "Does Bathilda need help?" he asked.

Jane nodded. "Carey thinks Bathilda is strange. We're worried about what Carey might do."

Kilmer held up one of his big hands. "Don't worry. I know Bathilda is not an ordinary baby — she's special. But everyone is special in one way or another."

Annie put her hand on Kilmer's shoulder. "We think your whole family is special. That's why we have to come up with a plan to make Carey leave Bathilda alone. I just hope we're not too late."

10

Chasing Bathilda

"Why don't you spend the night at my house again?" Annie suggested to Jane. "Maybe we'll think of something to help Bathilda before we go to bed."

Ben and Kilmer were busy patching the flat soccer balls when Ben suggested the same thing to his friend. "We can stay up late and watch scary movies," Ben told Kilmer.

Kilmer smiled. "I like scary movies. Sometimes I even see some of my relatives in them."

Later that night Ben, Kilmer, Annie, and Jane sat in front of the television set with a big bowl of popcorn. "I can't believe we're watching cartoons," Ben complained.

"There's nothing wrong with cartoons," Annie said, munching a piece of popcorn.

Ben groaned. "They stink. I wanted to watch *Revenge of the Killer Cobwebs.*"

Jane giggled. "Go look under your bed. There are plenty of cobwebs there."

"Really?" Kilmer asked excitedly.

"No," Ben said, "Jane is kidding."

The smile disappeared from Kilmer's face and he ate another handful of popcorn. Outside the kids heard a police car whiz by with its siren on.

"I wonder what's happening?" Ben said, going to the window to look out. Ben opened the window and leaned out. Kilmer went over to look, too.

Annie leaned close to Jane. "I like the police being around, but I hope they're not out there chasing Bathilda."

Jane shivered. "Do you really think Bathilda could be flying around Dedman Street?" she whispered.

Annie shrugged. "For all we know, she's out hunting for warm blood."

"Did you hear that?" Ben asked. The kids

got quiet and listened. They heard a strange growling and hissing sound.

"What is that?" Annie gulped.

Ben shut the window and snapped off the TV. "Let's go see," he suggested.

Annie shook her head. "No, let's just stay inside here where it's safe."

"Safe and boring," Ben said. "Real life is much more exciting than television. Let's go."

"Okay," Kilmer said.

The girls groaned, but they went to the door. Just before going outside, Annie grabbed a long scarf from a closet. She wrapped it around her neck, just in case Bathilda was flying around looking for something to bite. Jane took the flashlight from the closet.

"Ouch!" Jane yelled as they walked out into the backyard.

"What's wrong?" Annie asked. "Did you get bitten?"

Jane shook her head and held up an ac-

tion figure. "I stepped on this with my bare foot."

"Let me see that," Annie said. Jane flashed the light on the action figure and Annie pointed to the two holes in the figure's neck.

Jane gulped. "I don't hear anything," she said. "Why don't we go back inside?"

"Listen," Kilmer suggested.

Sure enough, the kids heard a hissing sound, followed by growling. "I don't like this," Annie said. "I'm scared."

"There's somebody under the tree house," Ben whispered. Without waiting, Ben rushed over and grabbed the figure under the tree.

"Help!" Ben screamed.

11

The Real Vampire

"Help me!" Ben yelled again. Jane fumbled with the flashlight and shined it under the tree.

Ben sat on the ground while Carey's huge dog licked his face. "Here's your vampire," Ben said. "He's trying to lick me to death."

"What are you talking about?" Jane asked.

Ben picked up his flattened soccer ball. "Chewy is the one who's been poking holes in all our balls and tires."

"Are you sure?" Annie asked. She turned on the porch light so they could see.

Chewy snatched the deflated ball out of Ben's hand and started chewing on it. Then he shook the ball back and forth before tossing it in the air.

Kilmer laughed. "I think he wants to play."

Jane kicked her newly patched soccer ball into the yard. Chewy ran after it. Ben got to it right behind Chewy and kicked it. Chewy chased it. The kids raced all around the backyard, kicking the ball and letting Chewy run after it. They were having a great time until Carey and her father showed up.

"What are you doing with my dog?" Carey yelled.

Ben stopped running. "We were just playing," he panted.

Carey put her hands on her hips. "I think you were trying to steal him," she accused. Then Carey pointed to Kilmer and looked at her father. "His little cousin ruined my tires."

Annie stomped over to Carey and pointed a finger in her face. "Listen here," Annie said. "I have some news for you. We've found out who has been putting all the holes in things and it isn't Bathilda."

Carey stuck her nose in the air. "Of course you would say that."

Jane walked over and stood beside Annie. "She's saying it because it's true."

Kilmer nodded. "Chewy is the one who ruined the balls and tires."

"That's a lie," Carey said, stomping her foot.

Carey's father came up behind her and put his hand on her shoulder. "Don't get upset, dear," he told her. "Maybe there's been some mistake."

Just then there was a loud pop and a hissing sound. Chewy bounded up with Jane's soccer ball in his mouth. He shook it back and forth, then tossed it up in the air. The flat ball landed with a plop. Chewy pounced on the ball and continued chewing it.

Carey's father cleared his throat. "Well, it seems we owe somebody a soccer ball."

"Make that two soccer balls, please," Ben said, holding up his flat ball.

Carey's father smiled. "Carey will bring

them to you tomorrow. We're sorry about the trouble."

Ben grinned. "It's okay. I liked playing with Chewy and I definitely like seeing Carey embarrassed."

Carey turned red. She grabbed Chewy by the collar before stomping away. Her dad waved and followed Carey home.

"Well, I guess that solves that mystery," Jane said.

"Maybe," Annie said, "but what's that flying around Ben's head?"

Ben took one look and ducked. "Look out!" he screamed.

12

Dracula

"When that bat swooped around you last night," Jane said, "I figured Bathilda was going to get you for sure."

Ben rolled his eyes. "Bats don't hurt people," he explained to Annie and Jane. The three kids sat in the tree house. Their eyes had dark circles under them and they couldn't stop yawning.

"They can if they're vampire bats," Annie told him.

"Nobody proved Bathilda was a vampire bat," Ben said. "If anything is a vampire, it's Chewy. But I don't care. He was fun to play with. I wonder if the coach will let Chewy play on our soccer team."

"Not the way that dog punches holes in the balls," Jane said.

"Maybe Carey will bring Chewy over so I

can teach him how to play soccer without poking holes in the ball," Ben said.

"You can't be serious," Jane said. "You don't really want Carey to come over, do you?"

"I'd rather take my chances with Carey than with whoever is in that weird black van," Annie said.

Jane, Ben, and Annie peeked over the edge of the tree house. A black van screeched to a halt, dead center in front of Hauntly Manor Inn.

A tall man with pale skin and black hair swooped out of the van. He was dressed entirely in black and moved so fast he looked like he flew up the sidewalk.

"Who's that?" Jane whispered.

"That must be Dracula himself," Annie whimpered. "I bet he came to get Bathilda."

"I hope he's not planning on staying," Jane said.

Annie gulped. "I don't think I could sleep knowing Dracula lived next door."

"The Hauntlys would never let anything

bad happen to us," Ben said, but his voice cracked when he said it.

"We're in luck," Jane said with a whoosh of air. She pointed to the front porch of the inn. The figure in black hurried from the inn and rushed down the cracked sidewalk. Bathilda clung to his neck. "Dracula must be in a hurry to get back to Transylvania."

"We have nothing to worry about," Ben said with a grin.

As they got into the black van, Bathilda spotted the kids in the tree and grinned. Annie was sure she could see Bathilda's baby eyeteeth. Annie shuddered and pulled her collar up high. "I hope you're right," she told Ben. "But just in case, I think I'll sleep in a turtleneck as long as the Hauntlys are our next-door neighbors."

"Then you better buy a bunch of turtlenecks," Jane said, "because I have a feeling the Hauntlys will be here for a long, long time!"

About the Authors

Marcia Thornton Jones and Debbie Dadey like to write about monsters. Their first series with Scholastic, **The Adventures of the Bailey School Kids,** has many characters who are *monsterously* funny. Now with the Hauntly family, Marcia and Debbie are in monster heaven!

Marcia and Debbie both used to live in Lexington, Kentucky. They were teachers at the same elementary school. When Debbie moved to Aurora, Illinois, she and Marcia had to change how they worked together. These authors now create monster books long-distance. They play hot potato with their stories, passing them back and forth by computer.

About the Illustrator

John Steven Gurney is the illustrator of both **The Bailey City Monsters** and **The Adventures of the Bailey School Kids.** He uses real people in his own neighborhood as models when he draws the characters in Bailey City. John has illustrated many books for young readers. He lives in Vermont with his wife and two children.

Creepy, weird, wacky, and funny things happen to the Bailey School Kids!™ Collect and read them all!

The Adventures of
THE BAILEY SCHOOL KIDS®

❑ BAS0-590-43411-X #1 Vampires Don't Wear Polka Dots $3.50
❑ BAS0-590-44061-6 #2 Werewolves Don't Go to Summer Camp .. $3.50
❑ BAS0-590-44477-8 #3 Santa Claus Doesn't Mop Floors $3.50
❑ BAS0-590-44822-6 #4 Leprechauns Don't Play Basketball $3.50
❑ BAS0-590-45854-X #5 Ghosts Don't Eat Potato Chips $3.50
❑ BAS0-590-47071-X #6 Frankenstein Doesn't Plant Petunias $3.50
❑ BAS0-590-47070-1 #7 Aliens Don't Wear Braces $3.50
❑ BAS0-590-47297-6 #8 Genies Don't Ride Bicycles $3.99
❑ BAS0-590-47298-4 #9 Pirates Don't Wear Pink Sunglasses $3.50
❑ BAS0-590-48112-6 #10 Witches Don't Do Backflips $3.50
❑ BAS0-590-48113-4 #11 Skeletons Don't Play Tubas $3.50
❑ BAS0-590-48114-2 #12 Cupid Doesn't Flip Hamburgers $3.50
❑ BAS0-590-48115-0 #13 Gremlins Don't Chew Bubble Gum $3.50
❑ BAS0-590-22635-5 #14 Monsters Don't Scuba Dive $3.50
❑ BAS0-590-22636-3 #15 Zombies Don't Play Soccer $3.50
❑ BAS0-590-22638-X #16 Dracula Doesn't Drink Lemonade $3.50
❑ BAS0-590-22637-1 #17 Elves Don't Wear Hard Hats $3.50
❑ BAS0-590-50960-8 #18 Martians Don't Take Temperatures $3.99
❑ BAS0-590-50961-6 #19 Gargoyles Don't Drive School Buses $2.99
❑ BAS0-590-50962-4 #20 Wizards Don't Need Computers $3.50
❑ BAS0-590-22639-8 #21 Mummies Don't Coach Softball $3.50
❑ BAS0-590-84886-0 #22 Cyclops Doesn't Roller-Skate $3.50
❑ BAS0-590-84902-6 #23 Angels Don't Know Karate $3.50
❑ BAS0-590-84904-2 #24 Dragons Don't Cook Pizza $3.50
❑ BAS0-590-84905-0 #25 Bigfoot Doesn't Square Dance $3.50
❑ BAS0-590-84906-9 #26 Mermaids Don't Run Track $3.50
❑ BAS0-590-25701-3 #27 Bogeymen Don't Play Football $3.50

❏ BAS0-590-25783-8 #28 Unicorns Don't Give Sleigh Rides $3.50

❏ BAS0-590-25804-4 #29 Knights Don't Teach Piano $3.99

❏ BAS0-590-25809-5 #30 Hercules Doesn't Pull Teeth $3.50

❏ BAS0-590-25819-2 #31 Ghouls Don't Scoop Ice Cream $3.50

❏ BAS0-590-18982-4 #32 Phantoms Don't Drive Sports Cars $3.50

❏ BAS0-590-18983-2 #33 Giants Don't Go Snowboarding $3.99

❏ BAS0-590-18984-0 #34 Frankenstein Doesn't Slam Hockey Pucks .$3.99

❏ BAS0-590-18985-9 #35 Trolls Don't Ride Roller Coasters $3.99

❏ BAS0-590-99552-9   Bailey School Kids Joke Book $3.50

❏ BAS0-590-88134-5   Bailey School Kids Super Special #1:
                        Mrs. Jeepers Is Missing! $4.99

❏ BAS0-590-21243-5   Bailey School Kids Super Special #2:
                        Mrs. Jeepers' Batty Vacation $4.99

❏ BAS0-590-11712-2   Bailey School Kids Super Special #3:
                        Mrs. Jeepers' Secret Cave $4.99

❏ BAS0-439-04396-4   Bailey School Kids Super Special #4:
                        Mrs. Jeepers In Outer Space $4.99

Available wherever you buy books, or use this order form

Scholastic Inc., P.O. Box 7502, Jefferson City, MO 65102

Please send me the books I have checked above. I am enclosing $_____ (please add $2.00 to cover shipping and handling). Send check or money order — no cash or C.O.D.s please.

Name _____

Address _____

City_____ State/Zip_____

Please allow four to six weeks for delivery. Offer good in the U.S. only. Sorry, mail orders are not available to residents of Canada. Prices subject to change.   BSK1098